Green Gardening and Composting

Molly Aloian

Crabtree Publishing Company

www.crabtreebooks.com

Author
Molly Aloian

Publishing plan research and development
Reagan Miller

Editor
Rachel Eagen

Proofreader and indexer
Wendy Scavuzzo

Design
Samara Parent

Photo research
Samara Parent

**Production coordinator
and prepress technician**
Samara Parent

Print coordinator
Margaret Amy Salter

Photographs
istockphoto: pages 18, 20, 21
Thinkstock: cover, pages 8, 14
All other images by Shutterstock

Library and Archives Canada Cataloguing in Publication

Aloian, Molly, author
     Green gardening and composting / Molly Aloian.

(The green scene)
Includes index.
Issued in print and electronic formats.
ISBN 978-0-7787-0262-7 (bound).--ISBN 978-0-7787-0276-4 (pbk.).
-- ISBN 978-1-4271-0559-2 (pdf).--ISBN 978-1-4271-9435-0 (html)

     1. Organic gardening--Juvenile literature. 2. Compost--Juvenile literature.
I. Title.

SB453.5.A56 2013   j635'.0484   C2013-905213-5
                                                                          C2013-905214-3

Library of Congress Cataloging-in-Publication Data

Aloian, Molly.
  Green gardening and composting / Molly Aloian.
       pages cm. -- (The green scene)
  Includes index.
   ISBN 978-0-7787-0262-7 (reinforced library binding) -- ISBN 978-0-7787-
0276-4 (pbk.) -- ISBN 978-1-4271-0559-2 (electronic pdf) -- ISBN 978-1-4271-
9435-0 (electronic html)
  1. Sustainable agriculture--Juvenile literature. 2. Composting--Juvenile
literature. I. Title.

S494.5.S85A66 2013
631.5--dc23
                                                      2013030087

Crabtree Publishing Company

www.crabtreebooks.com   1-800-387-7650

Printed in Canada/092013/BF20130815

**Published in Canada
Crabtree Publishing**
616 Welland Ave.
St. Catharines, Ontario
L2M 5V6

**Published in the United States
Crabtree Publishing**
PMB 59051
350 Fifth Avenue, 59th Floor
New York, New York 10118

**Published in the United Kingdom
Crabtree Publishing**
Maritime House
Basin Road North, Hove
BN41 1WR

**Published in Australia
Crabtree Publishing**
3 Charles Street
Coburg North
VIC 3058

Contents

Green gardening

Have you ever heard the phrase "green gardening"? What do you think it means? Green gardening is planting and growing a healthy garden that is good for the environment.

Growing green

In a green garden, **pests** and other animals are kept away from plants naturally, without the use of chemicals. Plants grow and stay healthy with the help of natural **fertilizer**. **Recycling** and **reusing** everyday things will also help keep your garden green.

Items from around your home can become part of your green garden.

Small and simple

Some green gardens are big and have a lot of different plants. But small green gardens, including window box gardens or pots on the porch or balcony, are just as much fun to grow. In fact, a small green garden is much easier to care for and to keep green and healthy. You can pay more attention to each of the plants that grow in a small green garden.

There are fewer weeds in a small green garden. Small gardens also need less water.

Start a green garden diary. Write down all the names of the plants in your green garden and how they change as they grow.

Help from birds and insects

Slugs, **aphids**, and other pests eat garden plants. Some people use **pesticides** to keep these animals out of gardens. Pesticides are bad for the environment. They pollute the land, water, and air.

Welcome ladybugs into your garden. They will find shelter among your plants and eat aphids and other pests.

aphid

Eating pests

In a green garden, birds eat slugs, caterpillars, and other pests that kill plants. Ladybugs eat aphids that suck the juices from plants. There is no pollution from pesticides. The birds and ladybugs have food to eat and plants are safe from pests.

Take Action!

Put up birdfeeders and nesting boxes in or around your green garden. You will attract birds, and they will feed on any pests living on or around your plants.

Natural pest control

There are other green ways to keep pests away from plants in your garden. Garlic, cooking oil, milk, baking soda, hot pepper sauce, and cayenne pepper are all foods that naturally **repel**, or keep away, pests without causing pollution.

Scattering crushed eggshells around plants will help keep slugs and snails away from your plants.

Spray away

Making natural pest spray is easy! In a spray bottle, mix one or two tablespoons of any of the foods shown below with water. Let the mixture sit overnight. Spray the mixture on the leaves of your plants every day to help keep pests away without harming the environment.

cayenne pepper

MILK

cooking oil

hot pepper sauce

garlic

From home to garden

Used, old, or broken items from your home can be reused and recycled in your green garden. You can grow plants in used food containers, used juice or milk cartons, old boots or shoes, an old wheelbarrow, and in old baskets.

Shallow plastic trays make perfect seed trays.

Used again

Using any of these unusual plant containers will make any garden more interesting and special. It also keeps these items from piling up in **landfills**.

Look around your home for interesting plant containers. Old buckets, empty soup cans, plastic tubs, and old cookie tins all make great plant containers.

Making compost

Compost is a mixture of waste, such as dead leaves or vegetable peels, which has broken down and changed into rich soil. People use compost as fertilizer in green gardens. It helps plants grow and stay healthy without harming the environment.

Compost is full of nutrients. Plants need nutrients to grow and stay healthy, just like you.

14

Take Action!

Which of the items on this page can be put into a compost bin? Which items cannot be put into the bin?

From kitchen to compost

All kinds of kitchen and yard waste, including fruit and vegetable peels, eggshells, coffee grounds, grass clippings, and dead leaves, will break down into compost. Meat, bones, milk products, and pet droppings do not break down and should not go in the compost bin.

Breaking down

The waste in a compost bin breaks down with the help of **bacteria** and other **organisms**. Worms and other **decomposers**, such as flies and millipedes, eat the rotting food and other plant material. It becomes moldy and smelly.

Worms help make compost. They eat the rotting food and yard waste and help change it into dark brown soil.

Changing into compost

Over time, the waste changes. It starts to smell fresh like dirt and turns into dark brown, nutrient-rich soil that is perfect for growing plants in a green garden. Keep adding waste, and you will continue to have more compost to fertilize your green garden.

Using compost

The compost will be ready to use in about six to nine months. Ask an adult to help you shovel out the compost and spread it all around your green garden. Be sure to dig from the bottom of the compost pile.

If you put your hand over the compost pile, you might feel heat coming from the compost. That just means the waste is breaking down and changing.

Take Action!

Collect rainwater in containers, such as a rain barrel, to water your plants. Save water by avoiding use of the tap or hose.

All natural

The compost will help flowers, fruits, and vegetables grow. Making compost is a great way to recycle waste and keep your garden healthy and environmentally-friendly.

Other green gardens

Some green gardens are on the roofs of buildings in cities. These gardens are called rooftop gardens. The plants have enough water, space, and sunlight to grow, but do not take up any space on the ground.

There are rooftop gardens and community gardens at schools, hospitals, and in neighborhoods.

Take Action!

Talk to your family or a teacher at school about starting a rooftop garden or a community garden in your city or school.

Part of the community

Community gardens are great for people who want a green garden, but do not have a backyard. A community garden is a garden that is cared for by a group of people. Working together to take care of the flowers, fruits, and vegetables builds a sense of community and a connection to the environment.

Grow your own

It is fun and easy to grow your own fruits and vegetables at home. Ask an adult to help you get started.

1 Choose where to start your garden. Window boxes, pots, or old watering cans can all be made into containers for indoor or outdoor green gardens. Just make sure your garden gets plenty of sunlight.

2 Plant your seeds. Dig small holes in the dirt, drop in the seeds, and then cover the holes with dirt. Watercress, radishes, lettuce, carrots, beans, strawberries, and tomatoes are easy to grow.

3 Water your plants. Collect rainwater in containers or a rain barrel and use it to water your plants instead of using water from the tap or hose.

4 Once your plants start to grow, you can make a garden diary to track how they change. Ask an adult to help you pick the fruits and vegetables when they are ready to eat. Try making a meal out of the food you grew.

Learning more

Books

Lay, Richard. *Green Kid's Guide to Gardening!* Looking Glass Library, 2013.

Scholl, Elizabeth. *Organic Gardening for Kids*.
  Mitchell Lane Publishers, 2009.

Siddals, Mary McKenna. *Compost Stew: An A to Z Recipe for the Earth*.
  Tricycle Press, 2010.

Websites

National Geographic: Green Guide Yard Interactive-
http://environment.nationalgeographic.com/environment/green-guide/home-garden/room-by-room/yard/

Going Green with Kids
http://www.kidsgardening.org/node/3868

8 Garden Projects for Kids
http://www.care2.com/greenliving/garden-activities-for-kids.html

Organic Gardening for the Whole Family
http://www.stonyfield.com/blog/organic-gardening/

Words to know

Note: Some boldfaced words are defined where they appear in the book.

aphids (EY-fidz) noun Insects that suck the juices from plants

bacteria (bak-TEER-ee-uh) noun Living things in soil, water, or matter that can break down and change other matter

compost (KOM-pohst) noun A mixture of waste, such as dead leaves or vegetable peels, that has broken down and changed into rich soil for plants

decomposers (dee-kuhm-POH-zers) noun Living things, such as worms, flies, and millipedes, that can break down waste

fertilizer (FUR-tl-ahy-zer) noun Substances added to soil to make plants grow

landfills (LAND-filz) noun Huge holes in the ground that are filled with garbage and then covered with soil

nutrients (NOO-tree-uhnts) noun Natural substances that help living things grow and stay healthy

organisms (AWR-guh-niz-uhmz) noun Living things

pesticides (PES-tuh-sahydz) noun Chemicals that kill or keep away insects, slugs, mold, weeds, and other pests that damage plants

pests (pest) noun Insects and other animals that some people believe are harmful

recycling (ree-SAHY-kuhl-ing) verb Changing or processing something to be used again, sometimes in a different way

reusing (ree-YOOZ-ing) verb Using something again

A noun is a person, place, or thing.
A verb is an action word that tells you what someone or something does.

Index